Future Energy

Water Power

Julie Richards

This edition first published in 2004 in the United States of America by
Smart Apple Media.

Smart Apple Media
1980 Lookout Drive
North Mankato
Minnesota 56003

Library of Congress Cataloging-in-Publication Data

Richards, Julie.
    Water power / Julie Richards.
    p. cm. — (Future energy)

    Includes index.
    Contents: What is energy?—Water as a source of energy—Where does water come
    from?—Using water energy—Water energy through history—Early water-power
    technology—Modern water-power technology—Harnessing water power—Turning
    water energy into electricity—Water power at work—Water power and the
    environment—Water power in the future—Advantages and disadvantages of water
    power.

    ISBN 1-58340-335-3
    1. Water-power—Juvenile literature. [1. Water power. 2. Renewable energy sources.]
    I. Title.
    TC147.R53 2003
    621.31'2134—dc21   2002044637

First Edition
9 8 7 6 5 4 3 2 1

First published in 2003 by
MACMILLAN EDUCATION AUSTRALIA PTY LTD
627 Chapel Street, South Yarra, Australia 3141

Associated companies and representatives throughout the world.

Edited by Anna Fern
Text and cover design by Cristina Neri, Canary Graphic Design
Illustrations by Nives Porcellato and Andy Craig
Photo research by Legend Images

Printed in Thailand

Acknowledgements
The author and the publisher are grateful to the following for permission to
reproduce copyright material:

Cover photograph: Glen Canyon Dam, courtesy of Corbis Digital Stock.

Art Archive, p. 15; A. Reffet—Explorer/Auscape International, p. 7; Australian Picture
Library/Corbis, pp. 21 (top), 22, 25; Coo-ee Picture Library, pp. 9, 10, 13; Corbis
Digital Stock, pp. 1, 27, 30; Getty Images, pp. 8, 16, 21 (bottom); Legend Images,
pp. 17 (top), 29; Jiri Lochman/Lochman Transparencies, p. 19 (bottom); Mary Evans
Picture Library, pp. 11, 12 (top); Nasa, p. 6 (top); Panos Pictures, p. 23;
Photolibrary.com, pp. 4, 5, 14 (top), 18, 20; Reuters, pp. 24, 26.

While every care has been taken to trace and acknowledge copyright, the publisher
tenders their apologies for any accidental infringement where copyright has proved
untraceable. Where the attempt has been unsuccessful, the publisher welcomes
information that would redress the situation.

Contents

Glossary words
When a word is printed in **bold** you can look up its meaning in the glossary on page 31.

What is energy?

Energy makes the world work. People, plants, and animals need energy to live and grow. Most of the world's machines are powered by energy that comes from burning coal, oil, and gas. Coal, oil, and gas are known as fossil fuels. Burning fossil fuels makes the air dirty. This is harmful to people and damages the environment.

Scientists are not sure how much longer fossil fuels will last. It depends on whether or not new sources of this type of energy are found and how carefully we use what is left. Scientists do know that if we keep using fossil fuels as fast as we are now, they *will* run out. An energy source that can be used up is called non-renewable. A renewable source is one that never runs out. The world cannot rely on fossil fuels as a source of energy for everything. We need to find other sources of safe, clean, renewable energy to power the machines we have come to depend on.

These are the fossilized remains of a fish. Fossil fuels are the plants and animals that died millions of years ago and turned into coal, oil, and gas.

Water Power

Water as a source of energy

Most of the Earth's surface is covered with water. Water gets its energy from movement. Rivers flow towards the sea. The oceans have tides that come and go from the shore. Moving water can travel faster than a car. The weight of a large amount of water moving at great speed can knock over houses and bridges and sweep them away as if they were toys. Moving water is a source of tremendous energy. It is kinder to the environment than burning oil, coal, or natural gas because water produces no poisonous gases or waste. Water is a renewable source of energy—it can be used again and again.

Moving water is a source of clean, renewable energy that can be harnessed to do work.

Fact file

Only about one percent of all the Earth's water is easily available freshwater. Ninety-seven percent is salty seawater and two percent is fresh water which is underground and locked inside glaciers and the ice at the North and South poles.

Where does water come from?

The Earth is the only planet in the solar system that has oceans and clouds made of water. The Earth was not always this wet. When the planet was forming, it was so hot that water did not exist at all. Scientists believe that, when the Earth cooled enough for clouds to form, it may have rained all over the world for hundreds of years. Great hollows in the Earth's surface filled with water to become oceans.

The darkest areas in this photograph of the Earth are the oceans. More than two-thirds of the Earth's surface are covered by oceans.

How water moves around the Earth

Water moves around the Earth through the water cycle. When the Sun shines, it warms the oceans, lakes, and rivers. Water droplets change into an invisible gas, called water vapor, which rises into the air. High up in the sky, the air is much cooler. When the water vapor hits this cooler air, it changes back into water droplets. The groups of water droplets that can be seen in the sky when this happens are called clouds. The water eventually falls back to Earth as rain, hail, and snow. Some falls back into the oceans, lakes, and rivers. Some falls on land and seeps into underground streams.

For more than three billion years, the Earth has been using the same water. It is reused through the water cycle and moves around the Earth in clouds, rain, rivers, and oceans.

The water cycle

Moist, warm air rises and then cools down to become clouds.

As the Sun warms the lakes and oceans, water turns into a gas (water vapor) and rises upwards.

Rain falls from clouds.

Some rain falls as snow on mountain tops.

Snow melts and finds its way into streams and rivers.

Rivers return water to the sea.

Some water sinks into soil and rocks.

Water comes to the surface of the Earth through springs and streams.

Water
Power

Natural water energy

Water is a very powerful force of nature. Without water, the Earth would not survive. The fact that few animals and plants live in or on the edge of the world's deserts shows us how important water is for living things. Moving water is powerful enough to carve through solid rock and send cliffs tumbling into the sea. Water is moved in nature by currents and tides.

A current is the direction in which water flows. Some currents flow faster than others. Oceans soak up some of the Sun's heat and spread it around the Earth through moving currents. Water always flows downhill. Rivers begin in mountains and flow down to the sea. In some places on a river, the rocks may have worn away to make a waterfall. Waterfalls were the first places people chose to use the natural energy of falling or moving water.

The natural energy of moving water carries heavy logs downstream to the sawmill.

Fact file

Niagara Falls, in the United States, is a very famous waterfall. Water pours over its edge at 1.4 million gallons (5.5 million l) per second.

Waves have carved their way through the cliffs, leaving these rocks standing alone.

Tides

Twice each day, the sea comes in and goes out again. This movement of water is called the tide. High tide is when the sea comes in. Low tide is when the sea goes out. Tides happen because the Sun and the Moon pull on the Earth like giant magnets. As the Moon travels around the Earth, it pulls most strongly on the oceans on the side of the Earth closest to it. This makes the oceans rise and fall in different places at different times. The height of the tides depends upon the positions of the Sun, Moon, and Earth. In the Bay of Fundy, in Canada, the difference between the height of the sea at high tide and low tide can be as much as 68 feet (21 m)—the biggest in the world.

The rubbing action of waves against some types of rock can wear the rocks away over thousands of years. Sometimes, the energy from the ocean is sudden and violent. Undersea earthquakes and volcanoes can **churn** the ocean into large, powerful waves called tsunamis. Tsunamis crash onto land, sweeping away everything in their path. One tsunami even carried a U.S. warship nearly 2 miles (3 km) inland.

Water Power

Using water energy

The natural energy from flowing rivers and ocean tides is used for transportation and farming.

Giant ocean waves and rivers bursting their banks show us the incredible strength of moving water. People could see there was a source of energy that could be useful to them if it could be harnessed. Natural water energy is not always available. It cannot be easily controlled, because the energy in water comes from movement. How fast water moves often relies upon other things, such as the weather and melting snow on high mountains.

During the 1800s, a more reliable source of energy called electricity became available. Electricity is made by burning coal in power stations. It is used to light buildings and power machines. Electricity can be made all the time so long as coal or oil is burned. Cables carry the electricity to wherever it is needed, and it can be switched on and off whenever people want. Today, the fossil fuels that are burned to make electricity are beginning to run low. Water energy will never run out. Scientists have worked out ways to collect, store, and use the power of moving water to make electricity.

Many countries rely on the energy of moving water to bring rich soil to their farms.

Water energy through history

People have used the energy of moving water for thousands of years for transportation, farming, and simple machines.

Ancient use of water energy

Farmers have always used rivers for **irrigation**. They dug ditches from the banks of rivers that ran alongside their fields. The water would flow from the river to where **crops** were growing. In some parts of the world, rivers flooded each year, spreading rich soil across low-lying land. As the water drained away, the farmers planted their crops and looked forward to a good harvest. They understood how important these floods were and prayed to their gods that the floods would come each year.

Waterwheels

The waterwheel was the first machine built by ancient people. A waterwheel is a wheel with paddles fixed around its rim. When the wheel is dipped in moving water, the water pushes against the paddles, turning the wheel. Some of the earliest waterwheels were invented by the ancient Greeks in 400 B.C. Most of the early waterwheels were used to turn huge stones that crushed grain into flour.

Waterwheels are one of the oldest forms of water power. This Syrian waterwheel is more than 500 years old.

This waterwheel was used by blacksmiths in France during the 1500s.

Modern use of water energy

Before machines were invented, animals did all the heavy work that people were not strong enough to do. The waterwheel was the first machine to be invented in ancient times, and people continued to use waterwheels in modern times. Most water-powered machines were used to grind grain. Some waterwheels were used to pump **bellows** that kept fires hot enough to melt metal so that it could be made into tools and weapons. Other waterwheels drove hammers that shaped the metal as it cooled.

However, water power was not always the most powerful and reliable source of energy. Not all rivers flowed fast enough to turn a waterwheel, and severe winter cold could make the rivers freeze over.

Steam-powered machines were invented during the 1700s. Heating water to steam produced a more powerful source of energy that could drive bigger and heavier machines. Wood and coal were burned inside boilers to heat the water. But wood and coal were expensive and difficult to transport to the machines, so waterwheels were still used most of the time.

Early water-power technology

A tidal barge on the
River Thames, in London,
in the late 1300s

Rivers and waterwheels were not the only sources of water power. Early **engineers** discovered that they could use the power of the ocean as well.

Tidal mills

Inventors began building tidal mills to harness the energy from the movement of the sea tides. The tides were not strong enough to turn a waterwheel, but the incoming water could be collected behind wooden gates and used later.

Tidal mills had some disadvantages. They could only be used twice each day. The tide does not come in and out at the same time each day, so the millers had to change their working hours each day, too. During the 1100s, about 100 tidal mills were working in Europe.

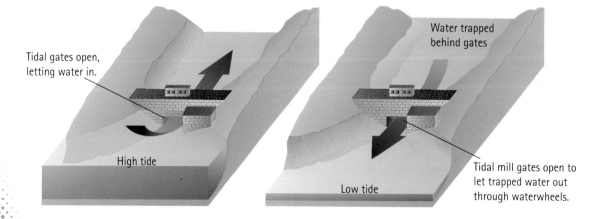

Tidal gates open, letting water in.

High tide

Water trapped behind gates

Low tide

Tidal mill gates open to let trapped water out through waterwheels.

A tidal mill

Water Power

Modern water-power technology

Most modern water-power technology revolved around the ability to turn water into steam. However, this all changed when electricity was harnessed in the 1800s.

Steam power

When water turns to steam, it swells quickly and violently. From 1712, steam engines were used to run simple machines such as mining pumps. Soon after, inventors began to harness the powerful force of steam to drive machinery on farms, in mines and factories, and as a form of transportation. They found steam-powered machines could do more work much faster than people. Richard Trevithick built the first **locomotive** engine in 1804. It pulled a load of 11 tons (10 t) and 70 people at a speed of 9 miles (15 km) per hour.

Electricity

Electricity began to replace steam power during the 1800s. Steam-powered machines and vehicles had to carry heavy loads of water and coal with them everywhere they went. The fires inside the boilers had to burn fiercely, or the supply of steam would stop—and so would the machine. Electricity could be made a long way away and sent along special cables to where it was needed. Turning on a switch was all anyone had to do to make electricity work. Today, nearly all the machines in the world run on electricity. Burning fossil fuels to make enough electricity is causing problems for the environment and people's health. There are ways to make electricity from the energy of moving water. Water power is a source of safe, clean, renewable energy.

A steam locomotive has a water-filled boiler which is heated to steam by burning coal.

Harnessing water power

The energy of water has been harnessed for the last 4,000 years. Even today, basic waterwheels are still used in some parts of the world. They can be used to run simple machines that grind grain or raise water from **wells**.

Waterwheel technology

There are two types of waterwheel:
- **vertical** waterwheels, which stand upright like a bicycle wheel
- **horizontal** waterwheels, which lie flat.

Vertical waterwheels

When the bottom of a vertical waterwheel is dipped in a river, the force of the moving water pushes against the paddles fixed around the wheel's edge. The water flows underneath it. The speed of the waterwheel depends on the speed of the water pushing against it. This type of waterwheel is called an undershot wheel.

An overshot waterwheel

When water runs onto the top of a vertical waterwheel, it is called an overshot wheel. Overshot waterwheels run faster, because it is the speed and weight of the water that turn the wheel.

There are two types of vertical waterwheel and one type of horizontal waterwheel.

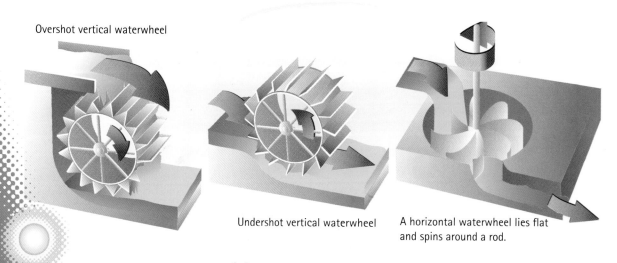

Overshot vertical waterwheel

Undershot vertical waterwheel

A horizontal waterwheel lies flat and spins around a rod.

Water Power

Horizontal waterwheels

A horizontal waterwheel lies flat and is driven by water falling from above through a pipe, or by a strong jet of water pointing at the paddles on the wheel rim.

Waterwheels were made from wood until 1776, when an English engineer called John Smeaton invented a metal wheel. By experimenting with the shape of paddles and the speed of the falling water, more **efficient** wheels were made. Inventors began to use metal-toothed wheels (called cogs) and chains to carry the energy from the waterwheel to the mill machinery. A **device** called the Burker's mill worked much like a garden sprinkler. It had a belt that took the energy from the spinning movement of the waterwheel and passed it on to a machine.

A waterwheel appears in this illustration of a Turkish bath house, painted in 1595.

Turning water energy into electricity

Moving water has energy that can be turned into electricity. Water is a clean source of energy because it does not release any harmful gases and chemicals into the air. Most of the energy used to make electricity comes from burning fossil fuels. The pollution made when fossil fuels are burned can be seen as a blanket of dirty, brown air covering our cities. **Acids** from the chemicals are carried inside raindrops. Acid rain eats away stone statues and poisons forests, lakes, and rivers.

Fossil fuels are a non-renewable source of energy. Once they have released their energy they cannot be used again. Water is a renewable source of energy because the water can be used again and again. Electricity can be made from moving or falling water. It can be made using the water from a rushing river or the action of ocean waves and tides.

These generators are part of a hydro-electric power station. They make electricity from moving water.

Water Power

The biggest hydro-electric power plant in the world is in the Snowy Mountains, Australia. There are 16 dams and seven power stations. The water in these pipes falls 1,500 feet (450 m) to the power station below.

Hydro-electricity

Electricity made from moving or falling water is called hydro-electricity. Hydro-electricity is made in a hydro-electric power station.

Hydro-electric power stations

A hydro-electric power station has a deep lake, called a reservoir. A reservoir is made by building a **dam** across a river at one end of a **valley**. The water builds up behind the dam and overflows, flooding the valley. Special gates called sluice gates are opened to let some of the water into a tunnel. As the water flows down through the tunnel, it gathers speed. The force of the fast-moving water spins the blades on a giant waterwheel called a turbine. A generator changes this spinning movement into electricity. Cables carry the electricity away to where it is needed. The water flows back into the river or dam.

Hydro-electric power stations make electricity from moving or falling water stored behind a dam.

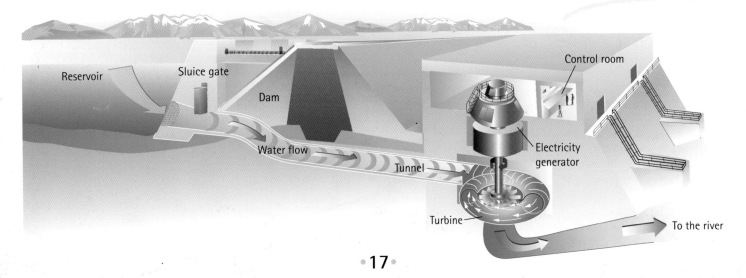

Storing water to make hydro-electricity

Water can be stored in a pumped storage station to make hydro-electricity when it is needed. A pumped storage station has two reservoirs: one below the power station and one above it. At night, when industry uses less electricity, the power station pumps water from the reservoir below it to the reservoir above it. During the day, when more electricity is needed, the water is allowed to flow back down into the lower reservoir. As the water flows down, it rushes through the power station and spins the turbines to make electricity.

The Dinorwig hydro-electric pumped storage station in Wales, in the United Kingdom, is known as Electric Mountain. It has 10 miles (16 km) of underground tunnels deep below Elidir Mountain. It took almost a million tons of concrete and 4,960 tons (4,500 t) of steel to build. Dinorwig's six generators stand inside one of the largest human-made caves in the world. When the turbines are switched on, they can reach maximum power in less than 16 seconds.

The pumped storage station in Dinorwig, Wales

Water
Power

Making electricity from waves

Ocean waves can be harnessed to make electricity. Waves are made by the tide or the wind blowing across the surface of the water. Ocean waves are full of energy. Far out at sea, they can only be seen as a ripple on the ocean's surface. But everywhere, the water is bobbing up and down.

Wave machines

A wave machine traps the energy of the bobbing movement of the waves and changes it into a spinning movement that can be used to drive an electricity generator. There have been many designs, but only a few test machines have been successful. Salter's Duck is a wave machine invented by a man named Stephen Salter. A row of Salter's Ducks uses the bobbing action of the waves to make electricity by squeezing water through the blades of a turbine. Salter's Duck is very efficient. It can change nearly all of a wave's energy into electricity.

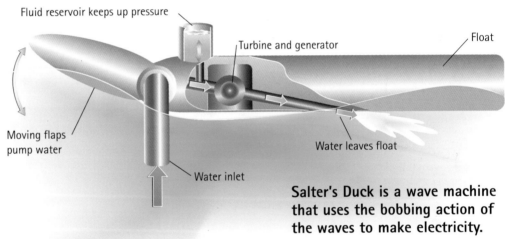

Fluid reservoir keeps up pressure

Turbine and generator

Float

Moving flaps pump water

Water leaves float

Water inlet

Salter's Duck is a wave machine that uses the bobbing action of the waves to make electricity.

Clams

Another type of wave machine, called a clam, works in a different way. A clam is a row of giant floating air bags. The bags are squeezed as passing waves bob up and down beneath them. Air inside the clam is squeezed from one bag to another. Turbines between the bags spin as the air is pushed through.

The energy of the ocean punches water through the holes in this rock so hard that it blasts high into the air. Water-column generators use the ocean's energy in a similar way.

Water columns

The most practical and useful wave machines have a moving column of water inside them. As the waves rise and fall, the water inside the column rises and falls too. When the water rises, it pushes air out of the top of the column. When it falls, it sucks the air back in. Each time this happens, the moving air spins a turbine. These wave machines are called **oscillating** (*OS-sil-lating*) water-column generators.

Scientists first make models of wave machines and test them in a water tank. The Salter's Duck and the clams are experiments, and can only produce small amounts of electricity. Wave columns are being built and tested along the coast of Norway. They need to be incredibly strong to survive the battering waves.

This wave machine in Scotland generates enough electricity to power 300 homes.

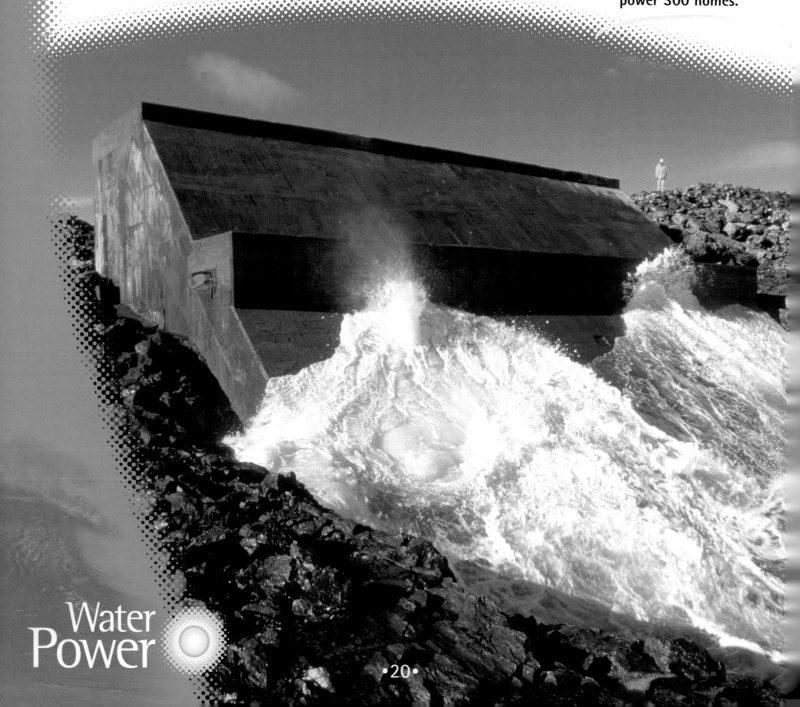

Water
Power

Making electricity from ocean tides

Enormous amounts of water move with the tides each day. Even a slow tide can generate electricity. Engineers use the same technology as was used for the tidal mills built more than 800 years ago. A modern tidal mill is called a tidal power station.

Tidal power stations

All rivers flow into the ocean. The place where a river meets the sea is called a mouth or estuary. A tidal power station has a wall built across an estuary. Open sluice gates along the wall allow the tide to flow in. The gates are closed when the tide is at its highest, trapping the water behind the gates. When the tide outside the gates drops, the gates open and the water inside rushes out into tunnels and through turbines.

Tidal power stations work best in places where huge ocean tides are squeezed into smaller rivers. When a lot of water is forced into a narrow **channel**, it travels much faster.

Tidal power stations do not cause any pollution, however **environmentalists** are worried that they may damage the environment in other ways. River estuaries are important feeding and nesting grounds for many birds. Tidal power stations change the natural flow of the tide and flood the areas where birds feed and nest. This may drive them away.

Tidal power stations may drive away birds that nest in river estuaries.

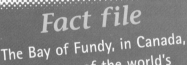

Fact file

The Bay of Fundy, in Canada, has some of the world's largest tides and produces giant waves 52 feet (16 m) high.

The biggest tidal power station ever built is across the mouth of the River Rance, in France. The river and the sea are separated by a wall 2,500 feet (750 m) long. The power station produces enough electricity to supply 250,000 homes. The water flows through 24 tunnels, each containing a turbine and a generator.

Water power at work

All moving water contains energy that can be used to generate electricity and do other work. Water power can be a useful source of clean, renewable energy. Water power does not pollute the environment with gases and **soot**, and it does not upset the weather or make people sick. Water power is a better choice of energy than the world's shrinking supply of polluting fossil fuels.

Steam turbines

Waterwheels are still being used today. Modern waterwheels are called turbines. The real power behind modern water-powered machinery is steam. Steam turbines are much simpler than the first steam engines. The first steam engines were driven by a **piston** that moved up and down. A steam engine needed to change the piston's movement into a spinning motion before it could be used to drive machinery. To do that, a complicated system of chains and belts was invented.

The enormous force of steam drives a turbine faster than any waterwheel could turn. Modern turbines can spin in both directions. This is very useful in tidal power stations and pumped storage stations, where water flows backwards and forwards. Unlike the old waterwheels, turbines must be sealed inside an airtight case, so the high-pressure steam cannot escape.

A steam turbine is a modern waterwheel driven by the force of water heated to steam.

Water Power

A micro-turbine generates power for a small village in Vietnam.

Power stations

Steam turbines drive generators to produce electricity in all kinds of power stations. Non-renewable fossil fuels such as coal, oil, and gas are burned in most power stations to make the steam that spins the turbines. The world's need for electricity is growing every year and fossil fuels are becoming scarce. Workers must go deeper to find fossil fuels and it is becoming more difficult and dangerous to bring these fuels out of the ground. Hydro-electric power stations only use water—a clean and renewable energy source. Hydro-electric power stations last longer than fossil-fueled power stations. They are non-polluting, easier to run, and not as expensive.

Hydro-electric power stations

Most hydro-electric power stations are very large and supply electricity to big cities. Hydro-electricity is also suitable for people living in **developing countries** or **remote** areas where there is no proper electricity supply and other sources of power may be too expensive. Although hydro-electricity is kind to the environment, building the dams can destroy the land and force people to leave their homes.

Fact file
Norway is a European country with high mountains and heavy rainfall. Ninety-nine percent of Norway's electricity is made in hydro-electric power stations.

·23·

The engine on a jet ski sucks water in and pumps it out as a powerful jet.

Water-powered transportation

Most of the ships and boats we have today are powered by engines that spin propellers. These engines use fossil fuels as a source of energy. Some crafts are powered by water, which is forced through narrow nozzles by powerful pumps. These nozzles are called water jets. If you have a garden hose with a nozzle attached to it, you will know that, if the water is concentrated into a narrow stream, it is much more powerful than when it sprays outward like a shower. If you put the hose on the ground, the force of the water makes the hose move about by itself. Water jets can move boats and jet skis about in much the same way.

Water jets

Water jets are driven by engines that use fossil fuels. However, the ships and boats that use water jets have a special shape that helps them to use less fuel and produce fewer poisonous fumes. It is possible that, in the future, water-jet engines will use cleaner, renewable energy such as **fuel cells**, **hydrogen**, or fuels made from rotting plant material.

The propellers used on ships and boats are easily damaged if they scrape along the **sea-bed** in shallow water. They can become entangled in weed, damage the water environment, and are extremely dangerous if swimmers are nearby.

Water-jet ships and boats do not need propellers. The water jet is used to steer the craft by moving the nozzle from side-to-side. Pumps beneath the craft suck in huge amounts of water and squeeze it into a narrower, faster jet. Some water jets could fill an Olympic swimming pool in 33 seconds!

Fact file
Shellfish have used squirting jets of water to move themselves about for millions of years.

Water Power

Water-jet tools

Water-jet tools use streams of water under high pressure to do jobs such as cleaning and cutting. Water is so powerful in nature, it can carve holes in rocks, wash away cliffs, and bring down roads and bridges. Concentrating a lot of fast-flowing water into a thin jet makes it powerful enough to do useful work.

Water-jet tools are used in **quarries** to cut through hard clay and separate precious metals such as gold from grains of gravel. Buildings and statues in polluted cities become covered in a thick crust of dirt from being surrounded by exhaust fumes and smog. High-powered water jets can remove the crust without the need for harsh chemicals that might damage some very old, delicate structures. Some water-cutting tools work at such high pressure that they can break very strong concrete. Sharp, rocky pieces can be added to the water to improve its cutting power. Workers drilling for oil and gas often use jets of high-pressured water to crack underground rocks so that the oil and gas are released.

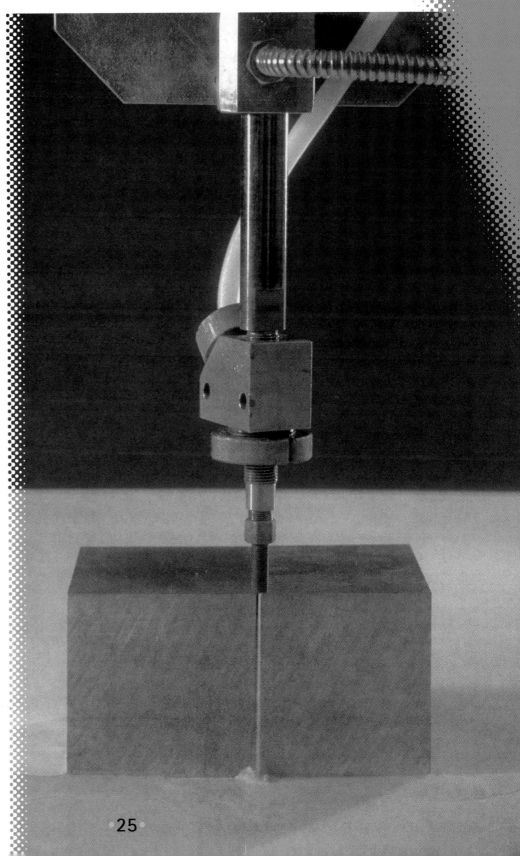

This high-pressure water-jet tool is being used to cut through a block of aluminum.

Water power and the environment

Although hydro-electricity has a lot of advantages for people living in developing countries and remote areas, there are some problems.

Environment

People in developing countries often rely on hunting, fishing, and farming for their living. Building the huge reservoirs and dams needed for large hydro-electric power stations can damage that type of environment. Enormous amounts of soil and rock are blasted with explosives and removed. Rivers are often **diverted**, and forests disappear beneath water. Animals are frightened away. If their homes and food supply are destroyed, they can never return.

People

People may have to leave their villages because the land will be flooded once a dam is built. In Mali, Africa, 10,000 people had to leave their homes because their village was flooded when the reservoir for the Manantali Dam was made. Sometimes, a river will be diverted. Fishers might have to carry their boats long distances to reach the new place of the river. Farmland may no longer receive the rich soil the river water brought with it and crops may die. These farmers and fishers will not be able to find other work. Most of them do not have enough schooling to be able to do other things. Some doctors are also worried that biting insects, such as mosquitoes, might live in the reservoirs and spread dangerous diseases, such as yellow fever and dengue fever, to people.

These people in Colombia are protesting because their village and land will be flooded to make a reservoir.

Smaller dams

Smaller dams can be more helpful to remote towns and villages than big hydro-electric power stations. Many remote villages are built near smaller rivers. Smaller dams can make use of these rivers without having to divert a much larger river. Small dams can supply drinking water for farm animals and irrigate crops, as well as providing electricity. A smaller turbine called a micro-turbine is used to generate the electricity needed to run important machines such as village water pumps.

Large dams are extremely heavy, because of the weight of the water they contain. This weight presses down hard on the rock layers beneath the Earth's surface. If the pressure is too great and the rock layers move, earthquakes can happen. Dams must be constantly checked for signs of cracking. Even the tiniest crack can mean big trouble. In parts of the world where earthquakes are known to happen, large hydro-electric power stations cannot be built.

Fact file

In China today, 90,000 small dams provide many small towns and some cities with most of their electricity.

The reservoir behind the Glen Canyon Dam, in the U.S., holds 10,000 million gallons (40,000 million l) of water.

Water power in the future

As fossil fuels run low, water power may become a more important energy source for the future. Tidal power and wave machines are still being developed. Many test machines have been battered and sunk because they are not strong enough to withstand the pounding of stormy seas. Warmer oceans trap and store a vast amount of the Sun's heat. Scientists are looking at ways to change this heat into electricity using a device called an ocean thermal energy converter or OTEC.

An OTEC uses warm seawater to heat a liquid and change it into a gas. The gas powers a turbine, which is linked to a generator that makes electricity. Cold seawater changes the gas back to a liquid so it can be used again. OTECs would also produce freshwater at the same time they made electricity. Some small OTECs have been built and tested. Like wave machines, they must withstand the constant pounding of waves. Sea plants and animals like to make their homes on and inside things left in the ocean. It is possible they could damage any device placed in the water.

Fact file

The first OTEC was built in 1929 off the coast of Cuba. It was not successful because it needed more electricity to run its pumps than its turbines produced. The idea of an OTEC was first suggested by a French scientist named Jacques d'Arsonval, in 1881.

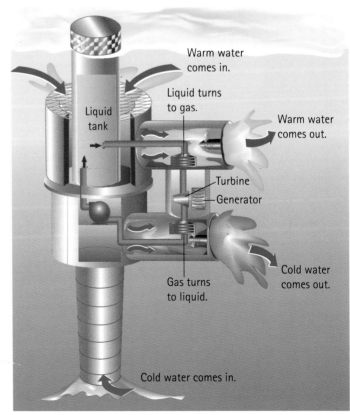

Warm water comes in.

Liquid turns to gas.

Liquid tank

Warm water comes out.

Turbine

Generator

Gas turns to liquid.

Cold water comes out.

Cold water comes in.

An OTEC uses heat from the sea to make electricity.

Water Power

Protecting the environment

Although water power is a natural source of clean, renewable energy for the future, the environment from where the water power is drawn still needs to be protected.

Dams

The area around a dam can be replanted with the same types of trees and grass that were there before. This protects the natural environment and encourages the animals and birds that once lived there to return after the dam is finished. Some power stations are built using the rock that has been broken up during blasting. This helps the power station to blend in better with its surroundings.

Rivers

A river that is diverted into dams and irrigation can lose so much water that, by the time it reaches the sea, it is just a trickle. The land around the river does not get enough water. The trees and plants die off. The animals leave because there is no food or water. As the trees die, the soil becomes loose and blows about. This is how deserts are made.

Global warming

The damage done to the environment by burning fossil fuels might be changing the world's weather. As the Earth gets warmer, some parts of the world are becoming so dry that people living there must constantly search for drinking water. If the Earth becomes hotter and drier, water power will be of little use to these people.

A great river that has been diverted into dams and irrigation can become just a trickle.

Advantages and disadvantages of water power

Fossil fuels are a non-renewable source of energy. If we keep using them at the current rate,
- coal will run out in 250 years
- oil will run out in 90 years
- gas will run out in 60 years.

There are other sources of energy that are cleaner, safer, and will not run out. Water power is a safe, clean, and renewable source of energy for the world's future power needs.

ADVANTAGES OF WATER POWER	DISADVANTAGES OF WATER POWER
• Water power does not cause pollution.	• It is expensive to build the dams and power stations needed to make hydro-electric power.
• Water power is useful for remote places. It can be tailored for use in individual households (using, for example, micro-turbines or smaller dams) as well as larger areas.	• Building dams and power stations can damage the environment and affect wildlife.
• Most of the Earth is covered with water, which is recycled through the water cycle, so it will never run out.	
• Moving water is always available when other natural energy sources such as the wind and the Sun are not.	
• Hydro-electric power stations are cheaper and easier to run than fossil-fueled power stations.	

Water rushes from a hydro-electric dam.

Water Power

30

Glossary

acids a type of chemical that can be harmful to people and the environment

bellows a device for blowing air onto a fire to make it burn more fiercely

channel a passage along which water flows

churn stir up and tumble about violently

crops plants grown for food

dam a wall built across a river to hold back water

developing countries countries that are beginning to use modern technology

device a machine or tool designed for a particular purpose

diverted to make something (e.g. the course of a river) change direction

efficient without waste

engineers people who design and build machines, roads, buildings, and bridges

environmentalists people who care for the environment

freshwater water that is not salty

fuel cells devices that produce electricity from a continuous chemical reaction inside them

generators machines that turn energy into electricity

glaciers frozen rivers of slow-moving ice

harnessed to be controlled and put to work

horizontal level with the horizon

hydrogen a colorless gas

irrigation watering crops by changing the path of water from a river using ditches

locomotive a railroad engine

oscillating moving backwards and forwards

piston a rod inside an engine that moves up and down

quarries places where stone is removed

remote very far away from other people

sea-bed the ground at the bottom of the sea

soot a black powder that rises with the smoke when coal is burned

steam water that has been heated until it turns into a gas

valley a piece of land between hills or mountains

vertical upright

wells holes drilled into the Earth

Index